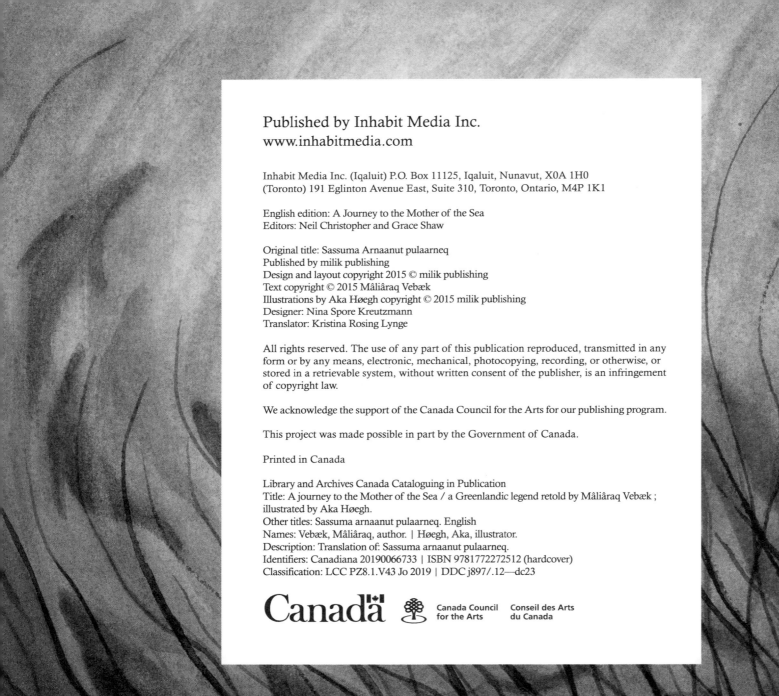

Published by Inhabit Media Inc.
www.inhabitmedia.com

Inhabit Media Inc. (Iqaluit) P.O. Box 11125, Iqaluit, Nunavut, X0A 1H0
(Toronto) 191 Eglinton Avenue East, Suite 310, Toronto, Ontario, M4P 1K1

English edition: A Journey to the Mother of the Sea
Editors: Neil Christopher and Grace Shaw

Original title: Sassuma Arnaanut pulaarneq
Published by milik publishing
Design and layout copyright 2015 © milik publishing
Text copyright © 2015 Mâliâraq Vebæk
Illustrations by Aka Høegh copyright © 2015 milik publishing
Designer: Nina Spore Kreutzmann
Translator: Kristina Rosing Lynge

We acknowledge the support of the Canada Council for the Arts for our publishing program.

This project was made possible in part by the Government of Canada.

Printed in Canada

Library and Archives Canada Cataloguing in Publication
Title: A journey to the Mother of the Sea / a Greenlandic legend retold by Mâliâraq Vebæk ;
illustrated by Aka Høegh.
Other titles: Sassuma arnaanut pulaarneq. English
Names: Vebæk, Mâliâraq, author. | Høegh, Aka, illustrator.
Description: Translation of: Sassuma arnaanut pulaarneq.
Identifiers: Canadiana 20190066733 | ISBN 9781772272512 (hardcover)
Classification: LCC PZ8.1.V43 Jo 2019 | DDC j897/.12—dc23

Canadä

Canada Council   Conseil des Arts
for the Arts   du Canada

A Journey to the Mother of the Sea

A Greenlandic legend retold by Mâliâraq Vebæk
Illustrated by Aka Høegh

A long time ago, the people of Greenland believed in the Mother of the Sea. She lived at the bottom of the ocean, where she ruled over all the creatures of the sea. She was all-knowing and very powerful.

From her dwelling on the ocean floor, she would send seals, whales, fish, and seabirds up to the surface for hunters to catch. That is why people called her the Mother of the Sea.

However, if people began behaving badly, she would become angry and withhold the animals. Then a shaman would have to be sent down to clean and comb her hair, which would become tangled and dirty as a result of people's misdeeds. She was so powerful that only the mightiest of shamans could visit her at the bottom of the ocean.

A shaman was a wise person who had supernatural powers and was both feared and revered. Shamans could cure the sick and predict the future. Only a few women became shamans, but those who did were more powerful than their male counterparts.

3

We shall now hear how it came to be that a feeble old woman went to visit the Mother of the Sea at her home on the ocean floor, and about the horrors and torments she had to endure on her way.

The old woman lived in a small village with her feeble old husband. Once, they had both been shamans, but as they had grown into old age, their powers had dwindled. Now, they were only useful for looking after children whose parents were away. If the children became too boisterous, the old couple would use their fading powers to make the floor tiles shake and vibrate, frightening the children into calming down.

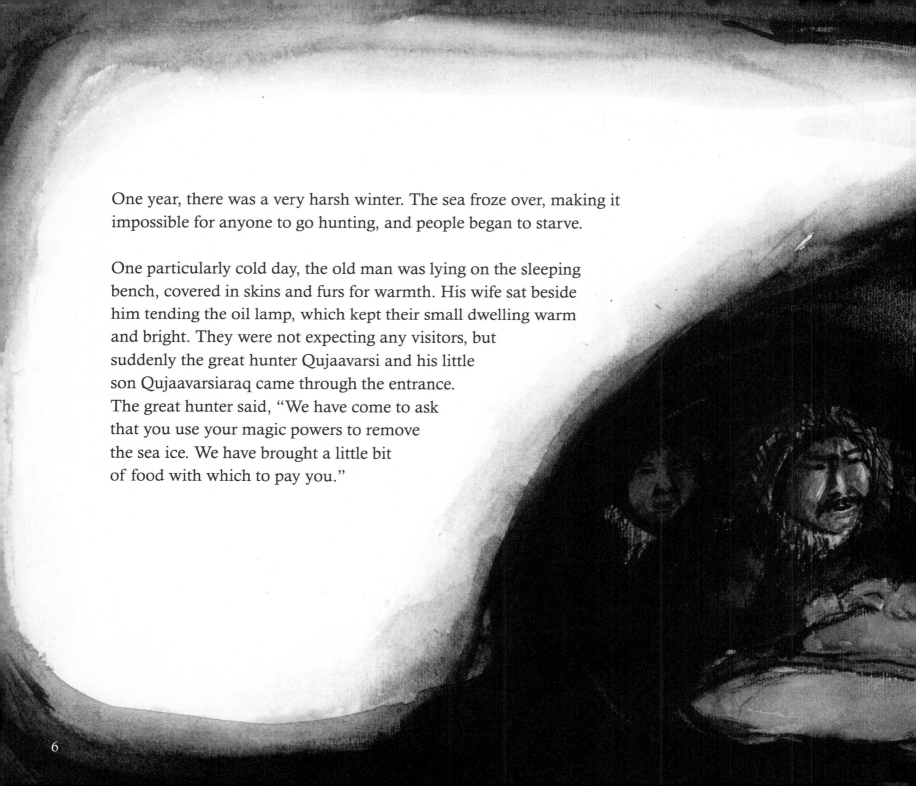

One year, there was a very harsh winter. The sea froze over, making it impossible for anyone to go hunting, and people began to starve.

One particularly cold day, the old man was lying on the sleeping bench, covered in skins and furs for warmth. His wife sat beside him tending the oil lamp, which kept their small dwelling warm and bright. They were not expecting any visitors, but suddenly the great hunter Qujaavarsi and his little son Qujaavarsiaraq came through the entrance. The great hunter said, "We have come to ask that you use your magic powers to remove the sea ice. We have brought a little bit of food with which to pay you."

"I'm sorry, but we can't do magic anymore," the old man said. "We are too old."

"We have heard that you use magic to make the floor tiles shake, scaring the children. If you can do that, you should also be able to remove the ice," the great hunter said.

"No, we cannot," the old couple replied. "We can't remove the ice; we are simply too old. Our powers have left us."

"My son had just learned to hunt seal when the ice came and covered the sea. Now he is bored and plagues me to ask you to make the ice disappear. You have to try! Besides," the great hunter continued, "we will soon be out of food."

The great hunter kept begging and pleading, and at last the old woman said, "We can try, but we are so old that it may be no use."

The great hunter and his son were very pleased that the old couple would at least try to remove the ice. "We must, however," the old couple said, "wait until it is dark to begin."

When you are waiting for something exciting to happen, time seems to pass extremely slowly. This was how it felt for Qujaavarsiaraq—to him, that afternoon felt like the longest afternoon of his life.

But finally, evening fell. The old couple ordered the oil lamp to be put out, because magic spells are only to be cast in complete darkness. When the lamp was out and darkness had claimed the tiny room, the old couple began to chant. They chanted for a very long time. Then the old man asked his wife, "Do you sense anything?"

"No, I do not sense anything," she answered. They kept on chanting.

"Do you sense anything?" the old man asked again.

"No, I do not sense anything. We are very old, so maybe nothing will happen," the old woman answered. They kept on chanting.

"Do you sense anything now?" the old man asked again.

"I don't know. Maybe. . . ." his wife answered, in a way that meant she was beginning to sense something.

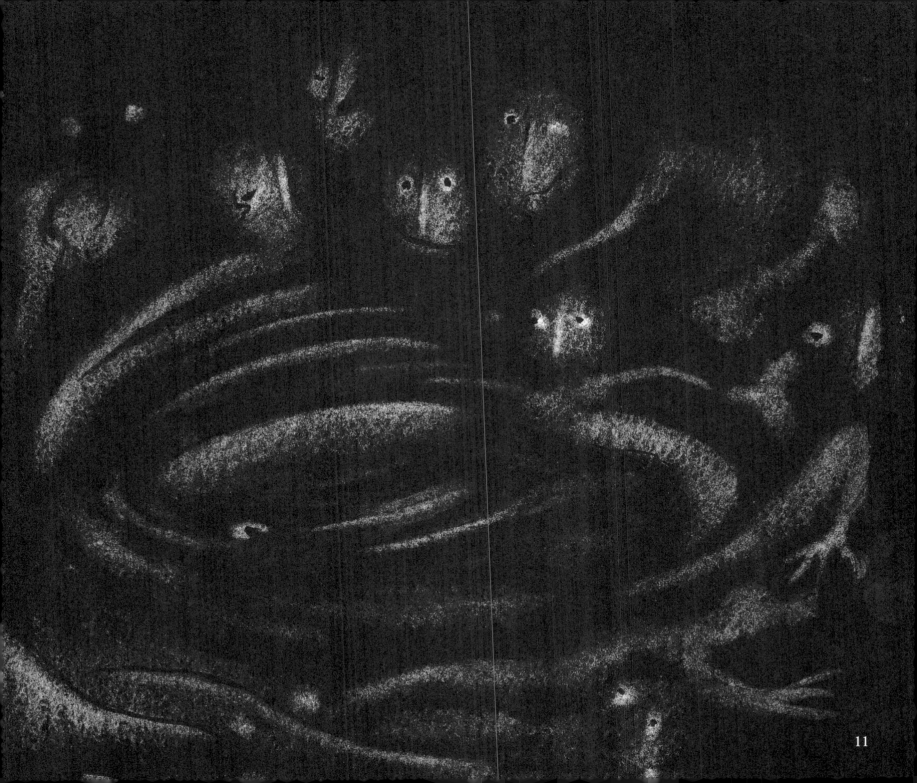

11

"That's how it is supposed to be," the old man said encouragingly, and they kept on chanting. "What do you sense now?"

"I see a polar bear walking on the ice and a walrus swimming underneath."

"That's good. That is how it is supposed to be," the old man said happily, and they kept on chanting.

"Now the polar bear is right outside our entrance, and the walrus is waiting down by the beach," the old woman said, and the couple stopped chanting.

Then the old man told his wife, "The polar bear will bite you and throw you down to the walrus. It will be painful, but you must not let it show."

The old woman suddenly disappeared through the entrance.

Outside, the polar bear was waiting. It bit the old woman and threw her down to the walrus, just as her husband had said. She landed straight between the large tusks of the walrus. It was painful, but she didn't let it show. Then she lost consciousness. The polar bear came down to the walrus, and together they swam out into the deep water. There, they ate the old woman and then parted ways.

The old woman became droppings from the polar bear and the walrus, floating down through the sea to settle on the ocean floor. There, the droppings transformed back into the old woman. How glad she was! The old woman was now all alone at the bottom of the sea. She could feel that she had grown very strong. Now she had to find the home of the Mother of the Sea and ask her to remove the sea ice so people could once again hunt for food. She started walking.

She walked and walked until she finally saw a large house up ahead. As she approached, she saw an enormous dog sitting on top of the dwelling. It growled loudly, but the old woman wasn't scared. She continued straight toward the entrance. And what an entrance! There was a great, gushing stream right in front of it, preventing strangers from entering.

On her way toward the house, the old woman's helping spirit had whispered in her ear, "When you arrive at the great, gushing stream by the entrance to the home of the Mother of the Sea, stand back and wait. Eventually, mats the size of *kamiit* soles will come floating down the stream. Use them to jump over to the entrance."

Now the old woman was standing by the great, gushing stream, waiting for the mats to appear as her helping spirit had foretold.

Sure enough, a mat the size of a *kamik* sole came floating down the stream at an alarming speed. She let the first one pass by and waited for the next. When the next mat appeared, she was prepared. As it passed right in front of her, she quickly jumped onto it and leaped to the opposite shore. In this way, she reached the entrance to the dwelling of the Mother of the Sea.

The old woman crept through the entrance and
entered the house of the Mother of the Sea.

What a sight!

On a bench sat an enormous woman with a thick
mass of long, tangled hair draped over her body.
This had to be the Mother of the Sea. She glared
angrily at her uninvited guest, and the old
woman became a little anxious. Then she
remembered that her helping spirit would
come to her aid, and she waited to see
what would happen next.

"Come here," ordered the Mother of the Sea. "You shall clean my hair!" Just as the old woman reached her, the great woman grabbed her with one hand and lifted her as easily as if she were a baby.

The Mother of the Sea tried to toss the old woman into the stream. But the old woman's helping spirit whispered, "Wrap your fingers around her hair. This will save your life." The old woman did as she was told and clung to the hair. Twice, the Mother of the Sea tried to throw the old woman into the stream, but both times she clung to the great mass of hair, her fingers wrapped around it just like her helping spirit had told her.

Realizing she couldn't shake off the old woman, the Mother of the Sea relented: "Very well then, clean my hair."

The old woman began to clean the hair of the Mother of the Sea very thoroughly, untangling it with a large comb made of bone. Then she carefully wiped the huge woman's face with a soft skin cloth dipped in the finest of oils. When she was done, the Mother of the Sea said, "Thank you. I have not been cleaned for a long time. Upon your return to land, you must tell your fellow villagers to take care of the ocean. When people do not care about the ocean and it becomes polluted, I get covered in filth and become unsightly and unkempt. Then I must keep the sea animals from the surface in order to make people change their ways. I must do this until someone comes down to clean me. Ask everyone to remember this. People must not think only of hunting and food."

Even though the old woman hadn't spoken of her mission, the Mother of the Sea knew of it and said to her, "Let me see what I can do for you—help me move my oil lamp." The lamp was very large and heavy. They both grabbed it and shifted it a little to one side. From beneath the lamp, great flocks of seabirds flew out of the house and up toward the ocean surface. "That's enough," said the Mother of the Sea, and they moved the lamp back into place.

23

"There is one more thing we must do," said the Mother of the Sea as she moved to the opposite wall. "Do you see that large door? Help me open it."

The old woman helped the Mother of the Sea open the large door, only to behold a strange creature, part animal, part human.

"You must mark it," said the Mother of the Sea.

"How am I to do that?" the old woman asked.

"Scratch a patch between its eyes with your fingernail."

The old woman obeyed, and a bare patch appeared between the creature's eyes. "That is good," said the Mother of the Sea. "This will be your husband's last catch. And for cleaning me, I thank you."

The old woman then departed, leaving the dwelling of the Mother of the Sea.

The old woman headed back toward her village, walking along the ocean floor. She was happy that she had succeeded in her visit with the Mother of the Sea. She thought about what the Mother of the Sea had told her while she was cleaning her great mass of hair: She was to tell the hunters not to go hunting as soon as the ice broke up, but to wait. After a couple of days, they could go hunting. The first catch was to be given to herself and her husband. The old woman remembered everything the Mother of the Sea had told her. Her journey home passed quickly as she was so very happy.

Suddenly, she found herself outside her own home. She called out as she crept through the entrance: "Light the lamp! All is as it should be." Everyone was very happy to see that she was back safe and sound, her husband the happiest of all. They all slept until the light of day.

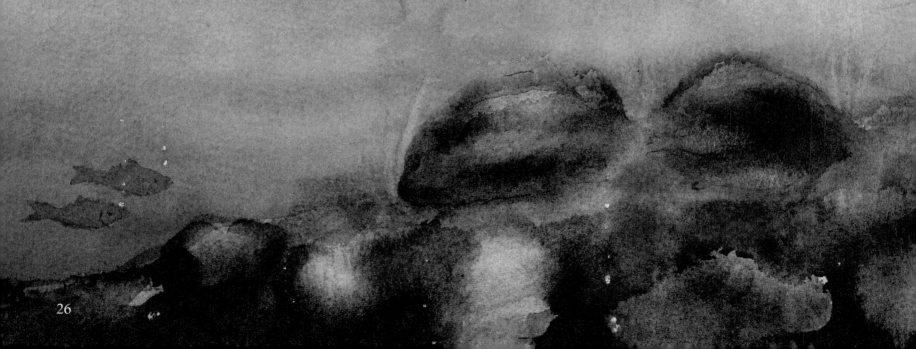

When they woke the next day, they heard the howl of a storm. Looking outside, they saw the ice breaking into a million pieces. Through its cracks, great flocks of seabirds emerged, and seals broke the surface of the water with their noses. The hunters hurriedly gathered their hunting gear and ran down to their kayaks. They had already forgotten the words of the Mother of the Sea, that they were not to go hunting straight away.

The hunters paddled out in their kayaks. However, every time they threw a harpoon, it fell straight down, right beside the kayak, as if it were broken. They returned to the village without a catch. They now believed the old woman's words and did not go hunting until she gave them permission to do so.

When she said it was time, the hunters went out. This time, they caught all the seals and birds they aimed for and only returned to the village when their kayaks were almost overflowing. They brought the largest and most beautiful seals and birds to the old couple, just like the Mother of the Sea had said they should. They also knew that the old man could not hunt for himself anymore. Everyone in the village had enough to eat, and the old couple never again lacked food.

One day, the old man said to his wife,
"I'm going out to hunt seal in my kayak."

The old woman smiled and thought to herself,
*What is he thinking? He hasn't been hunting for a very
long time, and his old kayak has been on its rack behind
our house for so long it is probably useless.* But she said nothing.

Before long, the old man returned from his hunt with a seal in tow.
The old woman went down to the beach and was amazed to see that
he had caught the finest seal in the entire ocean, with a pelt as beautiful
and smooth as silk. Then the old woman saw that the beautiful seal had
a bare patch between its eyes, and she thought of the strange creature
she had marked with her fingernail during her visit to the Mother of the
Sea. The Mother of the Sea had told her that it would be her husband's
last catch, and she now knew this to be true.

Everything had happened as foretold. And all this came to be because
the old woman, to save her village from starvation, had the courage to
undertake the dangerous journey down to the Mother of the Sea.

Glossary

For more Inuktitut pronunciation resources, including audio recordings of these terms, please visit inhabitmedia.com/inuitnipingit

kamiit (ka-MEET): many skin boots

kamik (ka-MIK): one skin boot

Iqaluit • Toronto

4·15

ARCHAEOLOGICAL MYSTERIES

SECRETS OF THE
TERRACOTTA
ARMY

TOMB OF AN ANCIENT CHINESE EMPEROR

BY MICHAEL CAPEK

Consultant:
Hanchao Lu
Professor of History
Georgia Institute of Technology
Atlanta, Georgia

CAPSTONE PRESS
a capstone imprint

Edge Books are published by Capstone Press,
1710 Roe Crest Drive, North Mankato, Minnesota 56003
www.capstonepub.com

Library of Congress Cataloging-in-Publication Data
Capek, Michael.
Secrets of the terracotta army : tomb of an ancient Chinese emperor / by Michael
Capek.
    pages cm.—(Edge books. Archaeological mysteries)
Includes bibliographical references and index.
Summary: "Describes the archeological wonders of the Terracotta Army, including
discovery, artifacts, ancient peoples, and preservation"—Provided by publisher.
ISBN 978-1-4765-9917-5 (library binding)
ISBN 978-1-4765-9926-7 (paperback)
ISBN 978-1-4765-9922-9 (eBook pdf)
1. Qin shi huang, Emperor of China, 259 B.C.-210 B.C.—Tomb—Juvenile literature.
2. Terra-cotta sculpture, Chinese—Qin-Han dynasties, 221 B.C.-220 A.D.—Juvenile
literature. 3. Shaanxi Sheng (China)—Antiquities—Juvenile literature. 4. Excavations
(Archaeology)—China—Shaanxi Sheng—Juvenile literature. I. Title.
DS747.9.Q254C37 2015
931'.04—dc23   2014007003

Developed and Produced by Focus Strategic Communications, Inc.
    Adrianna Edwards: project manager
    Ron Edwards: editor
    Rob Scanlan: designer and compositor
    Karen Hunter: media researcher
    Francine Geraci: copy editor and proofreader
    Wendy Scavuzzo: fact checker

Photo Credits
Age fotostock: Shigeki Tanaka, 25; Alamy: National Geographic Image Collection,
23, 24; Deborah Crowle Illustrations, 4; Dreamstime: John Chemycz, 11; Landov:
Reuters/Jason Lee, 26, Reuters/Jose Miguel Gomez, 27, UPI/Stephen Shaver, 28;
National Geographic Creative: Hsien-Min Yang, 19, O. Louis Mazzatenta, 5, 7;
Newscom: Robert Harding/Tim Graham, 13, ZUMA Press/Lan Shan, 6; Shutterstock:
Bob Cheung, 22, Craig Hanson, 16, Hung Chung Chih, 8, 12, 29, Inna Felker, 21,
lapas77, 3, 8–9 (back), 9 (front), 20–21 (back), Mario Savoia, cover, 1, milosk50, 4–5
(back), 10, 14–15 (back), 26–27 (back), pcruciatti, 17, raymoe81, 15

Design Elements by Shutterstock

Printed in the United States of America in Stevens Point, Wisconsin
042014   008092WZF14

TABLE OF CONTENTS

CHAPTER 1   A BURIED ARMY EMERGES 4

CHAPTER 2   REBUILDING AN ARMY 8

CHAPTER 3   AN ARMY FOR AN EMPEROR 14

CHAPTER 4   THE END OF QIN 20

CHAPTER 5   SAVING THE ANCIENT ARMY 26

GLOSSARY 30

READ MORE 31

CRITICAL THINKING USING THE COMMON CORE 31

INTERNET SITES 32

INDEX 32

CHAPTER ONE

A BURIED ARMY EMERGES

Farmers digging in the dark pit were frightened. For centuries they had heard about evil spirits that lurked beneath the soil in this field. Strange things had been seen here. Faces were said to have loomed suddenly out of the dirt when people had dug too deeply. Grasping hands had sometimes appeared. People had long whispered about these ghosts. Some thought they might be the guardians of the ancient emperor, whose tomb was nearby. Maybe it was the long-dead emperor himself!

LOCATION OF TERRACOTTA ARMY

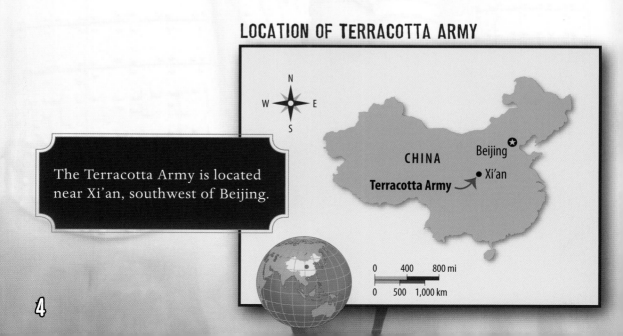

The Terracotta Army is located near Xi'an, southwest of Beijing.

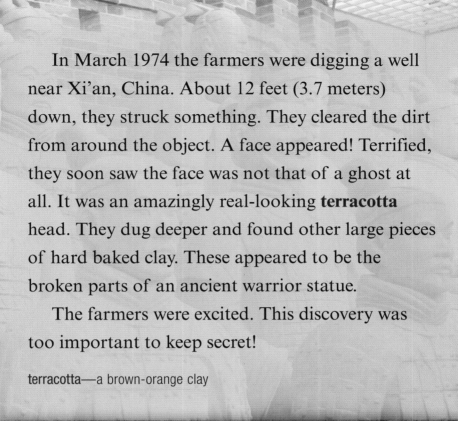

In March 1974 the farmers were digging a well near Xi'an, China. About 12 feet (3.7 meters) down, they struck something. They cleared the dirt from around the object. A face appeared! Terrified, they soon saw the face was not that of a ghost at all. It was an amazingly real-looking **terracotta** head. They dug deeper and found other large pieces of hard baked clay. These appeared to be the broken parts of an ancient warrior statue.

The farmers were excited. This discovery was too important to keep secret!

terracotta—a brown-orange clay

Workers gradually uncovered terracotta figures.

AN UNDERGROUND ARMY

Word of the amazing discovery spread fast. Soon **archaeologists** from all over China began to arrive. They were excited to see the terracotta pieces the farmers had found. The statue pieces were different from anything found in China before. The head appeared to be of an ancient warrior. Tests showed that the terracotta was more than 2,000 years old. The clay pieces had once been brightly painted, but the color faded quickly once exposed to light and air.

archaeologist—a scientist who studies how people lived in the past by analyzing their artifacts

Archaeologists unearth more terracotta warriors in 2009. Like during past excavations, they needed to be very careful not to damage the statues.

The archaeologists wondered if there might be more statues buried in the field. They dug many test holes in the ground. Nearly every place they looked had more statues and broken bits of terracotta. The buried statues were those of warriors in full battle gear. The archaeologists also found pieces of real weapons—swords, arrows, spears, and **crossbows**.

After months of careful digging, they found thousands of life-size warrior statues buried in the field. But who could have made this incredible army—and why?

CROSSBOWS

Crossbows have been used as weapons in hunting and warfare for thousands of years. The first crossbows were invented in China about 400 BC, and possibly as early as 2000 BC. Crossbows are smaller and easier to use than bows and arrows. Crossbows spread throughout the world and changed the way people fought wars.

crossbow—a weapon based on the bow and arrow

Rebuilding an Army

Months passed, and the dig grew wider and deeper. Searchers found **artifacts** in four pits. The pits had once been rooms in a building buried under 6 feet (1.8 m) of soil. The floors of the pits had been paved with bricks. Beneath the bricks were pipes to drain away any water that entered the rooms.

There were thousands of warrior statues standing in the pits. The workers also discovered pieces of terracotta horses and **chariots**.

Archaeologists have pieced together a bronze chariot from fragments.

But the number of warrior statues surprised the workers most. The warriors seemed to be everywhere. Nearly all of them were broken into small pieces. It took archaeologists and trained workers many months just to put one statue back together. Each ruined warrior had to be rebuilt by hand, like a huge jigsaw puzzle.

artifact—an object used in the past that was made by people

chariot—a light, two-wheeled cart pulled by horses

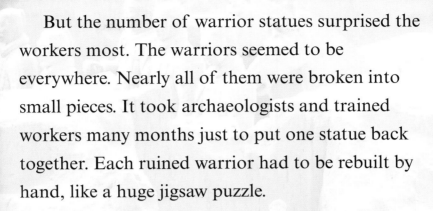

PIECES OF A PUZZLE

About 2,000 Terracotta warriors have been reassembled. The rest are still in pieces or lie buried. Experts think about 8,000 Terracotta warriors may have once stood in the pits.

WARRIORS OF ALL KINDS

Even before the warriors were put back together, researchers could tell that each one looked different. Some seemed older than others. Eyes and noses were different shapes. Each statue had its own hairstyle. There were many varieties of clothes and shoes on the warriors. Some smiled, while others seemed angry. Some had mustaches and beards. Others looked too young to have facial hair at all. Their sizes and poses were all slightly different as well.

Terracotta warriors

There were several kinds of warriors. The clothing and weapons on the statues showed what role each soldier played in the army. Statues of many common soldiers wore **tunics** and carried swords and shields. Some wore **fishscale armor**, which helped protect ancient Chinese warriors in battle. Warrior statues with longer beards were placed behind the ranks of soldiers. These statues were of older warriors, maybe officers. Most of the soldiers were standing, but some were kneeling. Many of the kneeling statues were archers designed to hold real bows and arrows or crossbows.

tunic—a long, loose-fitting shirt

fishscale armor—a kind of armor worn in ancient times made up of overlapping plates that looked like the scales of a fish

Most of the Terracotta Army figures held actual weapons. The weapons were not made of terracotta. They slowly fell apart after being exposed to moisture in the ground.

MORE MYSTERIES IN THE PITS

Years passed and the archaeologists kept digging. The search area stretched out across the field for more than 1 mile (1.6 kilometers). Everywhere they dug, they found more and more statues. One of the pits had statues of the army's highest officers. Their clothing was fancier, and these statues were taller than most of the others. Together a team of scientists searched for answers about the warriors buried in the pits.

Terracotta Army officer

MOLDS

Scientists have learned that all of the warrior statues were made from molds. Wet clay was put into wooden forms to make parts of the warriors' bodies—arms, legs, and heads. Then skilled artists took the clay out of the molds and added certain details to each piece. This was done by hand. The artists wanted to make each warrior different. All of the parts were then fired in **kilns**. The artists applied a special coating that sealed the terracotta pieces together into a solid statue. The final step was to paint the statues with bright colors.

kiln—a hot oven used to fire clay

Like the original builders of the Terracotta Army, historians today also use molds to make copies of the soldiers. These replicas are sometimes displayed in museums.

CHAPTER THREE

AN ARMY FOR AN EMPEROR

Over time the team of experts began to find answers about the terracotta figures. Old Chinese histories spoke of the burial of Qin Shi Huangdi (CHIN SHIH huang-DEE), the first emperor of China.

The emperor was one of the richest and most powerful rulers who ever lived. He ruled China more than 2,000 years ago. His army was one of the most feared in the world. None of the emperor's many enemies dared attack while his army was on alert. But ancient books said that Qin Shi Huangdi feared his own death. He wanted to have his army to protect him in the next life.

While he was still young, the emperor gave orders to build a vast underground tomb for himself. The workers were also told to make a perfect model of his whole kingdom.

Inside he wanted a model of everything he loved in order to live in comfort and safety in the next life. People in ancient China believed that objects buried with them would make them comfortable in the afterlife.

QIN SHI HUANGDI

Qin Shi Huangdi, the first emperor of China, was also known as Ying Zheng. He was only 13 when he became king of the state of Qin. At age 22 he led his army to victory over nine other states. His royal name, Qin Shi Huangdi, means "the first emperor of the Qin Dynasty."

statue of Qin Shi Huangdi

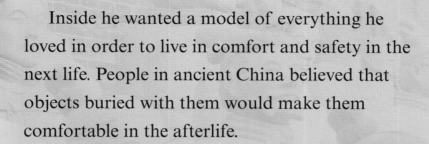

A CITY FOR SPIRITS

The emperor's army was the most important thing in the world to him during his life. Without it his many enemies would have attacked and taken away everything he had. Scientists agree that the Terracotta Army was Qin's way of taking his army with him after death.

There were also other things buried in the pits that the emperor valued. One was a huge garden. It had a park surrounded by many beautiful clay birds and animals. It even included a clay boatman and a real boat for the emperor to ride in. There was a stable with horses and **grooms**. Scientists also found a foundation of a grand palace. The emperor's whole tomb was meant to be a huge city. There he could live in luxury, just as he had while he was alive.

groom—a person who cleans, brushes, and cares for horses

After years of searching, archaeologists have discovered that the emperor's entire tomb covered more than 30 square miles (78 square kilometers). It included nearly 60 separate underground sections, including the Terracotta Army. Experts now see that all of the sections were part of Qin's master plan. He achieved the full-size underground "spirit city" he wanted.

ARCHAEOLOGICAL FACT

Historians say that more than 700,000 people worked on Qin's tomb while he was alive. The tomb was constructed between 228 and 246 BC. Many of the emperor's servants were killed at the time of his death so they could make the emperor comfortable in the next world.

Archaeologists excavate near Qin's tomb.

SKILLED WORKERS

Archaeologists have found skeletons of workers who built the tomb. They found that many workers had suffered broken bones and wounds. Often these injuries had been carefully treated as if by a skilled doctor. Tests done on bones and tooth enamel also showed many of the workers were well fed and healthy. The well-treated workers may have been artists or had special skills. Their creative work was probably seen as important. They had to be kept healthy if the tomb was ever to be finished.

Many thousands of workers created Qin's tomb.

ARCHAEOLOGICAL FACT

Nearly all the terracotta pieces have names carved into them. Experts believe the names are of the makers of the terracotta statues. These include both men's and women's names.

Many graves have been found near the pits. Some of the graves contain the bones of people killed in horrible ways. Historians believe these workers may have been killed to keep them from telling exactly where the emperor's spirit city was located. Some clearly were prisoners—chains and even clay tablets listing their crimes were found buried with them.

CHAPTER FOUR

THE END OF QIN

Records show that Emperor Qin Shi Huangdi died in 210 BC at the age of 50. As Qin had expected, China exploded into warfare immediately after his death. Hoping to take power for themselves, enemies attacked Qin's capital city. They killed his family and anyone loyal to him. They burned Qin's fine homes and palaces. Then they turned their anger on the parts of the emperor's tomb they could find.

Rebels dug tunnels to get into the underground chambers where the Terracotta Army stood guard. The looters stole many of the weapons.

ARCHAEOLOGICAL FACT

To warriors of ancient China, weapons as fine as those made for the emperor's army were more valuable than gold.

METAL WEAPONS

Artifacts found in the pits show how advanced the ancient Chinese were in making metal weapons. They knew the secret to making hard, strong metal weapons that would not break during heavy fighting. Modern science did not rediscover this secret until many centuries later.

Metal weapons on the Great Wall of China display the metalworking skills of the ancient Chinese.

LOOTING DAMAGE

It appears the rebels broke many of the Terracotta warriors. They also set fire to the wooden structure that had housed the soldiers. It fell, burning and crushing the figures, chariots, and other items inside. Chinese history books record this fire. It lasted for three months. Archaeologists figured out what had happened from clues they found as they dug. Tests of soil showed that the pits were full of charred wood. Also, many clay bricks and terracotta pieces were a dark red color and badly cracked. This damage could only have been caused by a very hot fire. Putting the evidence together, archaeologists came to understand what must have happened to the Terracotta Army.

burned and broken terracotta pieces caused by looters

The Army Is Reburied

Evidence shows that in the years following the attack on the emperor's tomb, the site changed. The ruined underground building and shattered army were slowly reburied when floods from the nearby Wei River brought silt and mud. Centuries of rain and wind laid down more dirt and dust. After 1,000 years no sign of the pits could be seen.

New rulers of China came and went, but the area where Qin made his burial grounds was left alone. After hundreds of years, people forgot about Qin and his magnificent army. Stories were told of the First Emperor's magnificent tomb complex, but not of the buried army. The world forgot that the warriors were there.

The area where Emperor Qin was buried is now heavily covered with trees and grass.

DON'T WAKE THE EMPEROR

The mound where the emperor was buried has changed too. At one time it was a step-pyramid. Earth was piled up and packed down in step-shapes. The hill was 394 feet (120 m) high. A chamber deep beneath the hill held the body of Qin and the treasures buried with him. Today the hill is smaller. **Erosion** has left it at a height of 210 feet (64 m).

erosion—the wearing away of land by water or wind

Emperor Qin is buried under a hill (foreground) that remains untouched.

There were many stories of rich treasure inside the tomb. But historians believe that no one ever disturbed the mound. One reason may be that the Chinese people have always honored the spirits of ancestors. Some people feared they would be haunted by ancient ghosts. Others simply respected the memory of the dead. Today most Chinese leaders think that great rulers, even those who were cruel and selfish, should be left in peace.

monument at Emperor Qin's tomb

ARCHAEOLOGICAL FACT

Historians claim that the inside of Emperor Qin's tomb is booby-trapped. Hundreds of hidden crossbows are said to be set and ready to shoot arrows at anyone who enters.

CHAPTER FIVE

SAVING THE ANCIENT ARMY

Research and digging continue on the Terracotta Army. Archaeologists are constantly making new discoveries. They believe many more amazing artifacts still lie buried, waiting to be discovered. But they have to be careful. They know that silk, wood, pottery, or paper buried deep underground will crumble once exposed to light and air. The emperor's tomb is nearby. But until science can find a way to safely explore the wonders of the tomb, it will have to remain sealed.

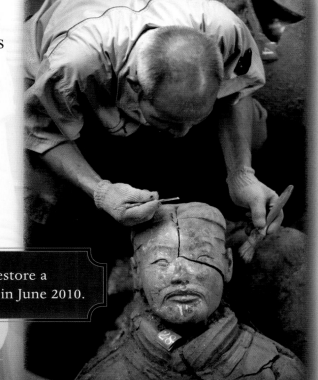

Technicians carefully restore a Terracotta Army statue in June 2010.

USING TECHNOLOGY INSTEAD OF DIGGING

Scientists are now using technology to see what is underground. A device sends sound waves deep into the earth. When the sound waves strike a hard object, they bounce back. They can be read by a computer and turned into an image. Scientists can create a picture of the entire underground site without having to dig!

technology device used for "seeing" underground

A Home for the Warriors

Millions of people visit the Terracotta Army every year at the Terracotta Warriors and Horses Museum near Xi'an, China. Visitors can walk around the pits and see the restored warriors. They can watch archaeologists at work restoring and studying the ancient figures.

The museum is also home to a library and exhibit halls. People from all over the world come to see many of the artifacts that have been found with the soldiers. Museum guides give demonstrations and explain how items were found and what they reveal about the past. Careful research by archaeologists and other scientists will preserve the Terracotta Army artifacts for future generations.

interior of Terracotta Warriors and Horses Museum

New Enemies Threaten

Great steps have been taken to protect the Terracotta Army for the future. But recent studies show that the warriors may be in serious danger. Scientists have learned that a better system of air control is needed at the museum. Pollutants such as mold and dust along with heat in the museum are causing the clay warriors to crack and break down. The air in the museum must be kept at a steady temperature and humidity level. It must also be filtered to remove harmful particles too small to see.

visitors outside the Terracotta Warriors and Horses Museum

GLOSSARY

archaeologist (ar-kee-AH-luh-jist)—a scientist who studies how people lived in the past by analyzing their artifacts

artifact (AR-tuh-fact)—an object used in the past that was made by people

chariot (CHAYR-ee-uht)—a light, two-wheeled cart pulled by horses

crossbow (KRAWS-boh)—a weapon based on the bow and arrow

erosion (i-ROH-zhuhn)—the wearing away of land by water or wind

fishscale armor (FISH-skale AR-muhr)—a kind of armor worn in ancient times made up of overlapping plates that looked like the scales of a fish

groom (GROOM)—a person who cleans, brushes, and cares for horses

kiln (KILN)—a hot oven used to fire clay

terracotta (ter-uh-KOT-uh)—a brown-orange clay

tunic (TOO-nik)—a long, loose-fitting shirt

READ MORE

Cohen, Jessica. *The Ancient Chinese.* Crafts from the Past. New York: Gareth Stevens, 2013.

Malam, John. *Terracotta Army and Other Lost Treasures.* Lost and Found. Irvine, Cal.: QEB Publishing, 2011.

Pilegard, Virginia Walton. *The Emperor's Army.* Gretna, La.: Pelican Publishing Company, 2010.

Roberts, Russell. *Ancient China.* Explore Ancient Worlds. Hockessin, Del.: Mitchell Lane, 2013.

CRITICAL THINKING
USING THE COMMON CORE

1. Using text from page 25, list at least three reasons why Emperor Qin's burial ground may have been left alone. Which reason do you think probably played the biggest role, and why? (Key Ideas and Details)

2. Find three examples in the book of what an archaeologist does. What do you think the advantages and disadvantages of working as an archaeologist would be? (Key Ideas and Details)

3. On page 18, the author suggests that the workers who appear to have been well cared for may have been artists or had special skills. What reasons does the author give to support this statement? Do you agree? Why or why not? (Integration of Knowledge and Ideas)

INTERNET SITES

FactHound offers a safe, fun way to find Internet sites related to this book. All of the sites on FactHound have been researched by our staff.

Here's all you do:

Visit *www.facthound.com*

Type in this code: 9781476599175

Super-cool stuff!
Check out projects, games, and lots more at
www.capstonekids.com

INDEX

archaeologists, 6, 7, 8, 9, 12, 17, 18, 22, 26, 27, 28
armor, 11
artifacts, 8, 21, 26, 28

chariots, 8, 22
clothing, 10, 11, 12
crossbows, 7, 11, 25

horses, 8, 16

looting, 20, 22

metal, 21

paint, 6, 13
pits, 8, 9, 12, 16, 19, 21, 22, 23, 28

Qin Shi Huangdi, 14, 15, 16, 17, 18, 20, 23, 24, 25
    burial mound of, 24, 25
    tomb preservation of, 28–29

reassembly of statues, 9, 13, 28

Terracotta Warriors and Horses Museum, 28, 29

weapons, 7, 11, 20, 21
workers (on Qin's tomb), 18, 19

Xi'an, China, 4, 5, 28

Ying Zheng, 15